For Andrew & Cheryl,
Who will be on the lookout together.
—S.K.

To big sister Luna, and her twin sisters Nora and Vada.
—L.M.

www.hmhco.com

The text of this book is set in Dante MT Std.
The illustrations are watercolor.

Library of Congress Cataloging-in-Publication Data

Names: Krensky, Stephen, author. | Munsinger, Lynn, illustrator.
Title: Dinosaurs in disguise / by Stephen Krensky ; illustrated by
Lynn Munsinger.
Description: Boston ; New York : Houghton Mifflin Harcourt, [2016] | Summary:
Did a comet kill off the dinosaurs, or are they masters of disguise,
hiding in plain sight all along?
Identifiers: LCCN 2015032157 | ISBN 9780544472716 (hardback)
Subjects: | CYAC: Dinosaurs—Fiction. | Humorous stories. | BISAC: JUVENILE
FICTION / Animals / Dinosaurs & Prehistoric Creatures. | JUVENILE FICTION
/ Imagination & Play. | JUVENILE FICTION / Bedtime & Dreams. | JUVENILE
FICTION / Humorous Stories. | JUVENILE FICTION / Nature & the Natural
World / Environment.
Classification: LCC PZ7.K883 Gq 2016 | DDC [E]—dc23
LC record available at http://lccn.loc.gov/2015032157

Manufactured in China
SCP 10 9 8 7 6 5 4 3 2 1
4500602469

And I can see why they stayed hidden
once some strange new creatures showed up.

And once the dinosaurs got used to blending in,

hiding soon became a habit.

That's why, even after all these years, we've never noticed the dinosaurs.

They're still in disguise.

Still, I'm sure I can find them
if I look hard enough.

There must be clues of one kind or another.

The way I see it, the dinosaurs have been hiding
for so long, they don't know what they're missing.
I'd really like to show them.

"You won't be sorry," I explain loudly.
"You just have to trust me."

For one thing, I'm sure they'd like easier ways
to hunt for dinner,

or the chance to go see old friends who don't live nearby.

And what about just relaxing at home?

Then again, the dinosaurs may feel uncomfortable
with the way things are right now.

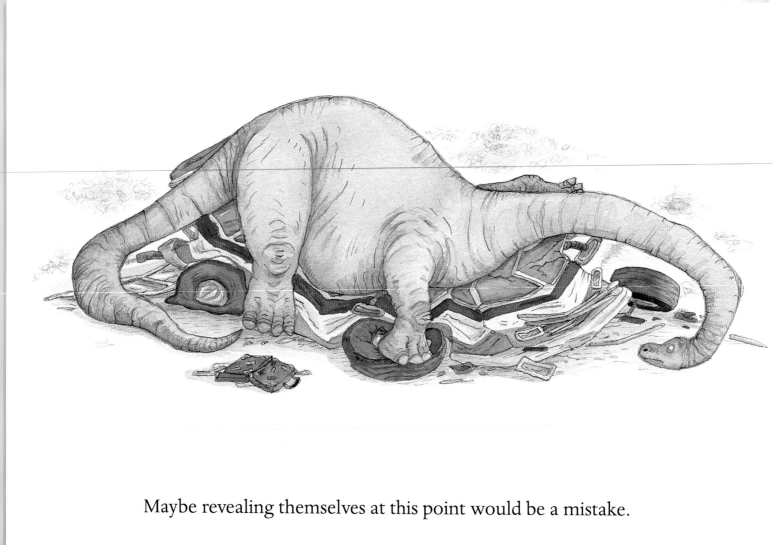

Maybe revealing themselves at this point would be a mistake.

Maybe we have some work to do first.